THE SPIDERWICK CHRONICLES

MALLORY ON GUARD

by Brooke Lindner
based on the screenplay by
Karey Kirkpatrick and David Berenbaum and John Sayles
from the books by
Tony DiTerlizzi and Holly Black

Ready-to-Read

Simon Spotlight
New York   London   Toronto   Sydney

SIMON SPOTLIGHT
An imprint of Simon & Schuster Children's Publishing Division
1230 Avenue of the Americas, New York, New York 10020
TM & © 2008 Paramount Pictures. All Rights Reserved.
All rights reserved, including the right of reproduction in whole or in part in any form.
SIMON SPOTLIGHT, READY-TO-READ, and colophon are registered trademarks of Simon & Schuster, Inc.
Manufactured in the United States of America
First Edition
2 4 6 8 10 9 7 5 3 1
CIP data for this book is available from the Library of Congress.
ISBN-13: 978-1-4169-4948-0
ISBN-10: 1-4169-4948-8

My name is Mallory Grace. A few weeks ago, I moved to Spiderwick Mansion with my mom and younger brothers. My great-aunt Lucinda used to live here. People said she believed her father, Arthur Spiderwick, had been taken by fairies. If you had asked me, I would have said that Aunt Lucinda must have been crazy.

The mansion did have a strange history. But there was nowhere else for us to go.

Before we moved, my brother Jared had been getting into a lot of trouble. He would get angry at the smallest things! I understood that he was mad that Dad didn't come with us, but we were all upset about that.

Mom needed us to be a family.
So I decided to take control and
help her deal with Jared. I would have
to be tough on Jared, no matter what he
did. I had to be strong for all of us.

When we first arrived at Spiderwick
Mansion, all I could say was, "Well,
it's big." It was so much bigger than
our old apartment in New York City.

Of all of us, Simon was the most excited to be there. He loves animals and I could tell he was thinking he could get more pets here. He had a cat, a few mice, and some tadpoles. I think he wanted something larger, like a dog or a cow. Maybe he would even find a wild animal in the woods and tame it.

We all soon found out that the creatures in the woods are not the kind you can tame.

We started unpacking, but Jared refused to get out of the car. Mom tried talking to him, but that didn't work. I knew what he needed: a good punch in the arm. That made him jump out and chase me with a stick.

Luckily, I'm on the fencing team,
so I was able to hold him off. I couldn't
let Jared mess this up. Mom needed this
to all work out.

I thought the mansion was pretty cool, even though it was musty. At least I got my own room—Simon and Jared had to share. Being an older sister can have its perks.

But after I unpacked, I noticed that my prized fencing medal was missing. I stormed down to the kitchen where

everyone was eating dinner.

"Where's my fencing medal, Jared?"
I said.

Of course, he shouted back, "I didn't
take your stupid medal!"

I didn't believe him. If Jared didn't
take it, who did?

A few minutes later, I heard a loud banging sound coming from downstairs. I ran downstairs to see what was going on. There was Jared, hitting the kitchen wall with a broom!

Mom followed me into the room. When

she saw Jared, she yelled, "Put that broom down. Now!"

Jared made up a lame excuse. He said he had heard something moving in the wall. I could tell by the tired look in Mom's eyes that Jared was going to drive her crazy.

I promised Mom that we would all help clean the kitchen so she could get some rest.

"Nice move, pinhead," I said to Jared.

Then from inside the wall, I heard a scratching sound. I grabbed the broom and gently tapped the wall to make the noise stop.

Instead, a huge chunk of the wall fell to the floor. Oops!

"Whoa," said Simon. "Check it out!"

I peered into the hole in the wall and saw what looked like a tiny elevator.

"It's a dumbwaiter," Simon quickly reminded me. He's good with words.

Jared slowly opened the door. Inside was a nest of small objects—like dollhouse furniture, lace, and money. But there were two strange things in there as well: Mom's car keys—and my fencing medal! How did that get in there? When I blamed Jared, he denied it.

But I said, "I don't know how you did it, but I know you did it, because you always do it."

Simon and I left Jared to clean up the mess. After all, he was the one who had started banging on the walls. Plus, I wanted to punish him for stealing my medal.

I went to bed, but woke up a few hours later. I heard the patter of small feet running away. I tried to roll over but my head would not move.

Then I reached my hand up to feel my head. My hair was tied to the bed! I screamed. Mom ran in to help. She was followed by Simon and, finally, Jared.

"Get him out!" I yelled, pointing at Jared. "He ruined my hair!"

"Do you really think I could tie knots in your hair without waking you up?" Jared said. "I've been reading in my room for the last two hours!"

Mom sent Jared back to his room and helped cut my hair from the bed. I was so mad that it took me a long time to get back to sleep.

The next morning, I was practicing my fencing with Simon when Jared came out holding an old book. He said it was written by Arthur Spiderwick, and he had found it in a secret study on the top floor of the house. The book had drawings of weird things like brownies, goblins, ogres, and trolls.

Jared asked us what the word "appease" meant. Simon told him it meant "to make nice." I told Jared if he was coming outside to "appease us," I wasn't interested. I was still mad at him for what he did to my hair.

THE COMMON HOUSE BROWNIES

Unusual organization of items is also common in houses with brownies. A brownie may alphabetize books by the middle initial of the authors' names or file records by the titles of -- favorite songs.

His shirt used to belong to a doll from my daughter's dollhouse.

One of my socks was used to make his pants.

Industrious themselves, even the gentlest of brownies hates laziness in others. If taken advantage of, or otherwise ill-used, the brownie may become a boggart.

Fiercely loyal, brownies will defend a home from burglars and goblins.

But Jared said, "I didn't do it. This did." He pointed to a picture in the book. He said it was a little creature called a brownie that turns into a boggart when it gets angry.

Brownie? Boggart? What in the world was Jared talking about? I began to think that he was making up stories instead of facing the truth.

But Simon was interested in what Jared was saying. As I said before, Simon always likes to learn about animals.

"Why is the brownie angry?" he asked.

Jared said that the pile of things we had found in the dumbwaiter was the brownie's home. The brownie had gotten angry when we messed it up. "That's why he tied your hair to the bed," Jared said.

In order to stop the brownie from turning into a boggart, Jared told us, we had to calm him down.

Okay. So Jared wanted us to say we were sorry to a fake animal. I began to wonder if Jared would blame the boggart every time he acted up. I was not going to fall for that.

Later, Mom went to work, and I was left in charge of my brothers. The morning was calm and quiet, until Jared ran into the kitchen. "They took Simon," he

cried. "They dragged him into the woods!"

"Give it a rest Jared," I said. "I don't believe you." But instead of yelling at me again, Jared ran out of the house. "Get back here!" I called. I watched as he vanished into the woods.

I started to get worried after a couple of hours. I couldn't lose Jared when I was in charge. Who knew what kind of trouble he was getting into now? I grabbed my sword and went outside to look for my brothers.

"Simon!" I called. "Jared! Where are you?" A few minutes passed. Then they both shot out of the woods and ran to the porch.

"There you are," I said to them. "You are so in trouble!"

"Run to the front door!" Jared yelled to me.

"Get inside the protective circle!" said Simon. What was he talking about? I stood still.

"Look out for the goblins!" Simon screamed.

Now Simon was playing Jared's game too!

Suddenly something scratched me on the arm. I swung my sword all over the place.

"They're short! Aim low!" Jared called. "Here, look through this!" He tossed a stone to me. I held the stone to my eye, and I could not believe what I saw.

Goblins—coming right at me!

Slashing my sword, I backed up to the mansion. Jared pulled me back, and the goblins stopped. It looked as if they were blocked by a wall and could not come any closer to the mansion. After a while, they scattered and ran back into the woods.

"Now do you believe me?" Jared asked. I nodded.

After that, I believed just about everything that Jared said. So I let him figure out a way to protect the mansion against the animals he had read about in Arthur Spiderwick's book. I knew that if anyone could come up with a plan, it would be Jared!